THE GREATEST GIFT

Y ou know the story of the Three Wise Men of the East, and how they travelled from far away to offer their gifts at the manger in Bethlehem. But have you ever heard the story of the Fourth Wise Man, who also saw the star in its rising, and set out to follow it?

THE GREATEST GIFT

The Story of the Other Wise Man

retold by Susan Summers   illustrated by Jackie Morris

walk
the way of wonder...
Barefoot Books

I n the days when Augustus Caesar ruled the Roman Empire and King Herod reigned in Jerusalem, there lived in the city of Ecbatana, among the mountains of Persia, a man named Artaban.

From the roof of his house, Artaban could look out over rising battlements of black and white, crimson and blue, red and silver, to the hill where the emperor's palace glittered above the city of Ecbatana like a jewel. Around his house grew a wonderful garden filled with flowers and fruit trees, watered by rushing streams and made musical by countless birds.

High above the tallest trees in the garden stood a tower, and from its window a lamp often shone late into the night, for it was here that Artaban worked. He was a follower of the faith of Zoroaster, studying the eternal struggle between the forces of good and evil, and exploring the secrets of nature – above all, the secrets of the night sky.

Artaban had three friends, Caspar, Melchior and Balthazar, and for all four men, knowledge of the stars was the highest form of learning.

One spring night, the four companions were looking up at the sky when they observed two great planets draw together in the sign of the Fish and a new star shining more brightly than any they had ever seen.

The men knew from their studies that this star signified the birth of a great teacher who was to be born among the Jews. There and then, they decided to follow the star. They arranged to meet up together at a place far away by the Temple of the Seven Spheres in Babylon; from there they would set out with a caravan of supplies and follow the star to Jerusalem, to pay homage to the child.

Quickly Artaban arranged his affairs. He sold his beautiful house with its fragrant gardens, and he bought three jewels – a sapphire, a ruby and a pearl – to carry as a tribute to the newborn child. On the eve of his departure, he said farewell to his old father, and knelt to receive his blessing.

Before dawn, even before the first bird had awoken, Artaban went down to the stable where Vasda, his favourite horse, stood saddled and bridled in her stall, shaking her bit and pawing at the ground impatiently. He swung himself into the saddle and was soon riding swiftly westwards: he had to reach the Temple of the Seven Spheres on the appointed night, and the journey was long and hard.

Artaban knew Vasda's strength, and pushed forward, riding late into the night and starting long before sunrise every morning. Each evening, as soon as the sun sank behind the hills, the bright new star shone down on him.

Finally, after ten days and ten nights, he saw before him the great walls of Babylon. At last! In three hours time he would be at the Temple of the Seven Spheres.

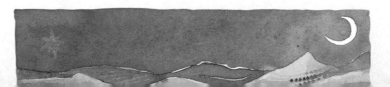

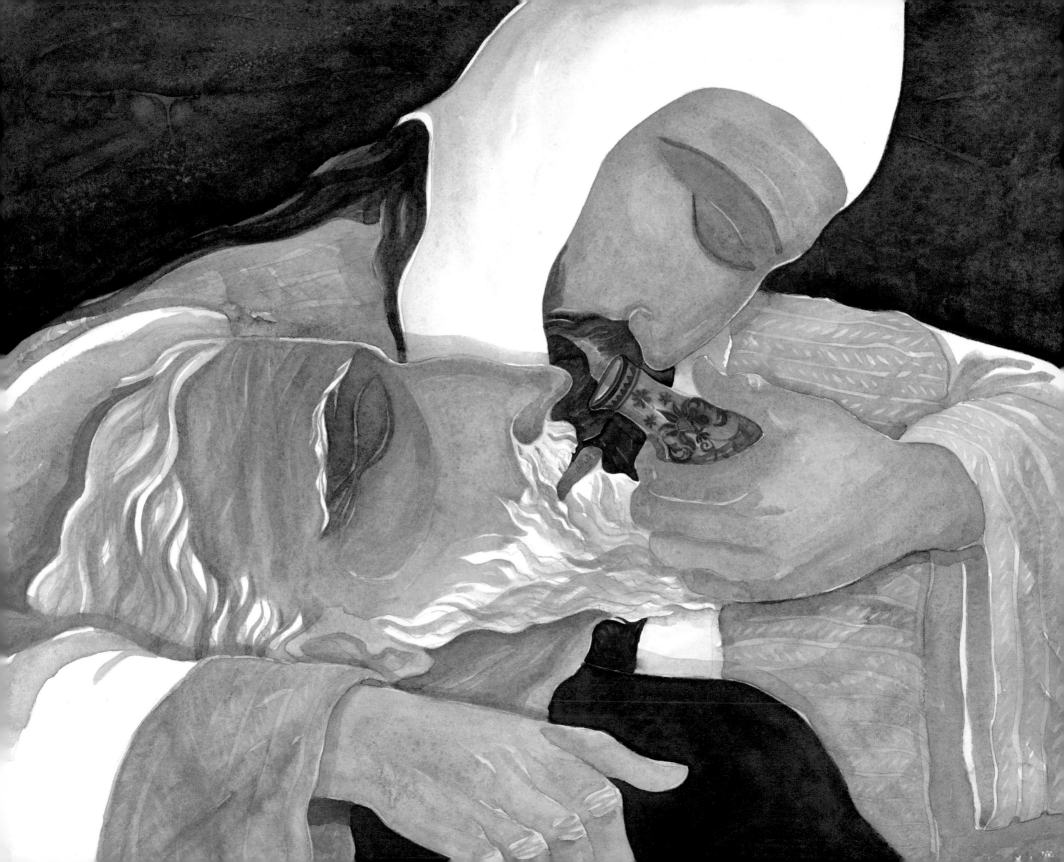

As they trotted past a grove of date palms outside the
city walls, Vasda started. She lowered her head and
gave a soft whinny, then stood stock-still, quivering
in every muscle, before a dark object lying in the shadow.

Artaban dismounted. In the dim starlight he could see the
figure of a man lying across the road. He leant down to
touch the man's head. The man gave a ghostly sigh and
clutched at his robe with long, bony fingers.

Artaban's heart leapt to his throat. The man needed help –
but how could he stop tonight, of all nights?

'God of truth and purity,' Artaban prayed, 'direct me in the
holy path, the way of wisdom which you know better than
any mortal.'

Then he fetched water, mixing it with some of the healing
herbs which he always carried. He laid the sick man's head
in the crook of his elbow and slowly poured the liquid into
his parched mouth. Hour after hour he poured, a little at a
time, then waited and poured again.

At last the sick man's strength returned.

'Who are you,' he asked, 'and why have you brought back
my life?'

'I am Artaban, of the city of Ecbatana, and I am going to
Jerusalem in search of one who is to be born King of the
Jews. I dare not stay with you any longer, for the caravan
that has been waiting for me may depart without me. But
see, here is all that I have left of bread and wine, and here is
a potion of healing herbs.'

The sick man raised his trembling hand solemnly to heaven.
'May the God of Abraham and Isaac and Jacob bless you and bring you peace! Now take heed: the Messiah will not be born in Jerusalem but in Bethlehem of Judah. May the Lord bring you in safety to that place, because you have had pity on me and saved my life.'

It was already past midnight. Artaban rode quickly across the silent plain, but when he reached the Temple of the Seven Spheres, he could find no trace of his friends.

Then, by the edge of a terrace, he saw a little cairn of bricks and under them a piece of parchment. He caught it up, and read: 'We can delay no longer. We go to find the King of Kings.'

Artaban stared out across the desert. 'How can I reach Judah,' he asked himself, 'with no food and a tired horse? I must return to Babylon, sell my sapphire and buy camels and food for the journey. I may never catch up with my friends. Only God knows whether I shall miss the King of Kings because I stopped to help a dying man.'

So Artaban returned to Babylon, where he sold his glittering sapphire and his beloved horse Vasda in exchange for a caravan of camels. Then he set out across the dreary desert.

Dark ledges of rock rose up around him like the bones of ancient monsters. Shifting hills of treacherous sand skirted his route. By day, a fierce heat blistered the earth, so that no living thing could move; by night, jackals prowled and barked in the distance and an icy chill fell over the dunes. But he pressed on, faithfully following the bright new star until, as the sick man had told him, it shone above the village of Bethlehem, in the land of Judah.

Artaban drew near the village, full of hope. Now at last he could give his pearl and his ruby to the King! But the streets were deserted, and he wondered whether the men had gone up to the hill pastures to bring down their sheep.

Then, from the open door of a stone cottage, he heard someone singing softly. He entered, and found a young woman singing her baby to sleep.

Yes, the woman told him, three strangers from the East had appeared a few days earlier. They had said that a star had guided them to the place where Joseph of Nazareth was lodging with his wife and her newborn son; and they had paid great reverence to the child and given him many gifts.

'But,' she went on, 'the travellers have disappeared again, and they say the man from Nazareth has fled to Egypt with his family. Now there seems to be a spell over the village. People even say that Roman soldiers are coming to enforce a new tax - and the men have driven our flocks and herds high up into the hills to escape it.' Artaban listened to her gentle voice, and the baby reached up to touch his face.

Suddenly there came a noise of wild confusion in the streets, a shrieking and wailing of women's voices, a clashing of swords and a desperate cry: 'The soldiers! The soldiers of Herod! They are killing our children!'

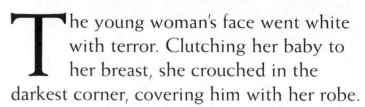

The young woman's face went white with terror. Clutching her baby to her breast, she crouched in the darkest corner, covering him with her robe.

Artaban strode over to the doorway. The tip of his white cap almost touched the lintel. When the soldiers reached the cottage, Artaban summoned their captain, and said: 'I am alone here, and I will give you this jewel, if you will leave me in peace.'

Then he showed the ruby, glistening in his palm like a great drop of blood. The captain's eyes widened with greed and he grabbed the jewel. 'March on!' he cried. As the soldiers left, Artaban turned to the east and prayed:

'God of truth, forgive my lie! I have said the thing that is not, to save the life of a child. And now two of my gifts are gone. Shall I ever see the King of Kings?'

But from the shadows behind him came the woman's voice, saying:

'Because you have saved my little one, the Lord bless you and keep you; the Lord let His face shine upon you and be gracious unto you; the Lord give you peace, now and always.'

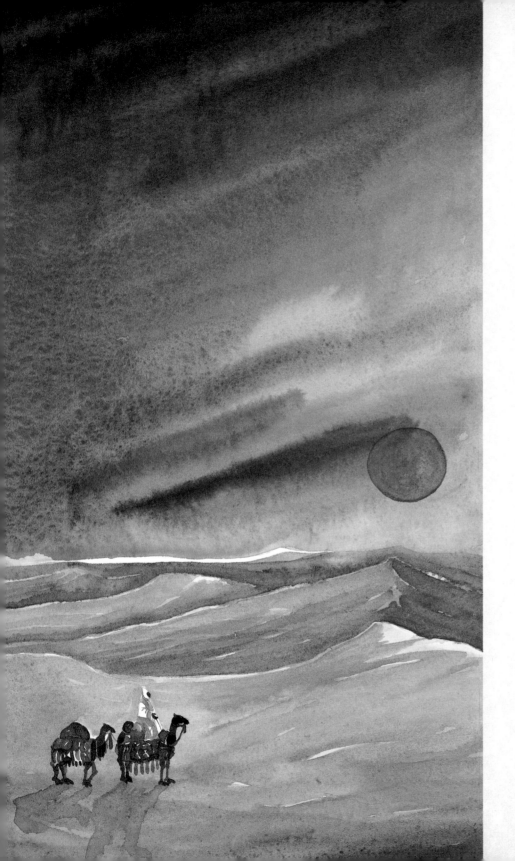

So Artaban left with the woman's blessing and made his way to Egypt, asking everywhere for news of the family from Bethlehem. But he could find no trace of them. By now, the star had vanished from the night sky, and he had no idea where to continue his search. So he went to a wise old Hebrew rabbi to seek advice.

'My son,' said the Rabbi, 'our scriptures foretold that the King of Kings would be despised and rejected by men. He will not be found in a palace, nor among the rich and powerful. If you seek him, look among the poor and the lowly, the sorrowful and the sick.'

The years passed, and Artaban travelled on, always searching in the poorest places for the family from Bethlehem. He passed through towns where people were crying with hunger; he passed through cities where they were dying of plague. And though he found no King of Kings to worship, he found many to help. Wherever he went, he fed the hungry and clothed the naked; he healed the sick and he visited those in prison; and his years went by more swiftly than a weaver's shuttle that darts back and forth through the loom, while the web grows and the invisible pattern is completed.

From time to time, he would stop and take out his pearl, the last of his gifts, and as he gazed on it, he would wonder whether he would ever meet the King of Kings.

Thirty-three years had passed since Artaban had first seen the star and set out on his journey. Now, worn and weary, he travelled to Jerusalem to make one final search.

He arrived during the season of the Passover, and the city was thronged with people who had come for the feast. But this year, there was a strange sense of foreboding in the air. All around Artaban, sandals clattered and thousands of bare feet shuffled over the stones as the crowds were swept along to the Damascus gate.

'What is happening?' asked Artaban.

'Haven't you heard?' replied a young man. 'There is going to be a crucifixion. Two robbers are to be crucified, and another man, a man called Jesus of Nazareth. They say he has said and done many wonderful things, and everyone loves him greatly. But the priests and the elders say he must be killed, because he calls himself the Son of God.'

T hen Artaban knew that this must be the King of Kings for whom he had been searching all these years. His heart thumped and his mind raced. Perhaps if he offered his pearl to the Roman Governor, Pontius Pilate, he might save the man's life!

He hurried towards the Damascus gate. But just beyond the entrance to the guard-house, a troop of soldiers came down the street dragging a young girl with a torn dress and dishevelled hair. As Artaban paused to look at her, she broke away from the hands of her tormentors and threw herself at his feet.

'Have pity on me!' she cried, 'Save me! My father was a follower of Zoroaster, and I see from your dress that you are of the same faith. Now my father is dead, and I am to be sold as a slave to pay for his debts. Help me, please!'

Artaban looked on the girl and trembled. For a third time, he had to choose between keeping his jewel as a gift for the King of Kings, or surrendering it to save a fellow human being. Yet he knew that to rescue this helpless girl would be a true deed of love.

Artaban took his priceless pearl from its pouch and placed it in the girl's hand:

'Here is your ransom, daughter! It is the last of the treasures I was keeping for the King of Kings, who is now to be crucified.'

As he spoke, the sky grew black and tremors ran through the street, which heaved like someone in pain. Houses rocked; stones fell and crashed into the street; dust clouds filled the air. The soldiers fled in terror, reeling like drunken men, and Artaban and the girl took refuge beside the wall of the guard-house.

The earth gave one final shudder, and a heavy tile, loosened from the roof, fell and struck Artaban on the temple.

As the girl bent over him, fearing that the old man was dead, there came a voice through the darkness, very small and still, like music sounding from a distance. The voice said:

'Peace be with you, Artaban. When I was hungry, you gave me food. When I was naked, you clothed me. When I was in distress, you comforted me. As often as you did these things to the least of my children, you did them for me.'

A calm radiance lit up the face of Artaban, and a long, last sigh of relief left his lips. His journey was ended. At last he had found his King.

Afterword

In Christian cultures, the visit of the three wise men, or the Magi, to the infant Jesus is celebrated every year on 6 January, the feast of the Epiphany. According to tradition, each of these wise men came from a civilisation which had a deep understanding of astrology. After they have presented their gifts to the infant Jesus at the stable in Bethlehem, the three wise men are warned in a dream to return home by a different route – and this is the last we hear of them. But many writers have been inspired by the notion of a fourth wise man, who also saw the star heralding the birth of Jesus but did not reach Bethlehem in time.

One of the most popular accounts in English of the adventures of a fourth wise man was written over a hundred years ago by Henry Van Dyke and was published as 'The Story of the Other Wise Man'. *The Greatest Gift* is based on this story, which follows the adventures of a Zoroastrian devotee called Artaban. The Zoroastrian faith flourished in the Middle East at the time of the birth of Christ, and astrology was an important aspect of the tradition.

A central aspect of the story of the Magi, and of later stories about the fourth wise man, is the emphasis placed on the Messiah as a teacher whose message would not only be important to the Jewish community into which he was born but to other traditions as well. For each of the wise men who saw the star understood that it signified the birth of a teacher with a universal message. Henry Van Dyke's story emphasises this theme, for Artaban actually lives and practises the teachings of Jesus, dedicating himself to a life of service as he searches for the King of Kings, and not discriminating against people belonging to different races or holding different belief systems from his own. In the spirit of the Henry Van Dyke story, *The Greatest Gift* echoes this message, at the same time showing how we can turn disappointment to good account; how the power of faith can transform our lives; and how our outer journey through life is mirrored by the inner journey of the soul.

Barefoot Books 124 Walcot Street Bath BA1 5BG

ISBN 1 902283 70 8